They Only See the Outside

poems by Kalli Dakos • illustrated by Jimothy Oliver

Magination Press • Washington, DC
American Psychological Association

To Kristine, John, Sarah, Scott, Katie, Dave, and to all

the children who will join our family one day—KD

**Books for Kids From the
American Psychological Association**

Poems copyright © 2021 by Kalli Dakos. Illustrations copyright © 2021 by Jimothy Oliver. Published by Magination Press, an imprint of the American Psychological Association. All rights reserved. Except as permitted under the United States Copyright Act of 1976, no part of this publication may be reproduced or distributed in any form or by any means, or stored in a database or retrieval system, without the prior written permission of the publisher.

With thanks to Laura Cinkant—KD

"Introducing a New Me" and "Ode to My Stress Ball" from PUT YOUR EYES UP HERE AND OTHER SCHOOL POEMS by Kalli Dakos. Text copyright © 2003 by Kalli Dakos. Reprinted with the permission of Simon & Schuster Books for Young Readers, an imprint of Simon & Schuster Children's Publishing Division. All rights reserved.

"Don't Tell Me," "Something Splendid," and "They Only See the Outside" from DON'T READ THIS BOOK, WHATEVER YOU DO! : More Poems About School by Kalli Dakos. Text copyright © 1993 Kalli Dakos. Reprinted with the permission of Simon & Schuster Books for Young Readers, an imprint of Simon & Schuster Children's Publishing Division. All rights reserved.

"J. T. Never Will Be Ten" and "Were You Ever Fat Like Me?" from IF YOU'RE NOT HERE, PLEASE RAISE YOUR HAND by Kalli Dakos. Text copyright © 1990 Kalli Dakos. Reprinted with the permission of Simon & Schuster Books for Young Readers, an imprint of Simon & Schuster Children's Publishing Division. All rights reserved.

"Countdown to Recess," "Homework," "The Most Important Time," "Four Wishes," and "The Book That Made Danny Cry" copyright © 1996 by Kalli Dakos. Originally published in THE GOOF WHO INVENTED HOMEWORK: And Other School Poems by Dial Books.

"They Put a Band-Aid on My Head" copyright © 2010 by Kalli Dakos. Originally published in I HEARD YOU TWICE THE FIRST TIME: Poems for Tired and Bewildered Teachers by BookSurge Publishing.

Magination Press is a registered trademark of the American Psychological Association. Order books at maginationpress.org, or call 1-800-374-2721.

Book design by Rachel Ross
Printed by Worzalla, Stevens Point, WI

Library of Congress Cataloging-in-Publication Data
Names: Dakos, Kalli, author. | Oliver, Jimothy, illustrator.
Title: They only see the outside / by Kalli Dakos ; illustrated by Jimothy Oliver.
Description: Washington, D.C. : Magination Press, [2021] | "American Psychological Association." | Summary: "A selection of poems on mental health topics including emotions, bullying, failure, illness, war, immigration, and goodbyes"—Provided by publisher.
Identifiers: LCCN 2020030373 (print) | ISBN 9781433835193 (hardcover)
Subjects: LCSH: Mental health--Juvenile poetry. | Children's poetry, American.
Classification: LCC PS3554.A414 T44 2021 (print) | DDC 811/.54—dc23
LC record available at https://lccn.loc.gov/2020030373

Manufactured in the United States of America
10 9 8 7 6 5 4 3 2 1

Contents

Introducing a New Me   1

Don't Tell Me   2

On the Day My Dog Died   3

Talking to the Mirror in the Bathroom   4

We Giggle the Same   5

The Fight   6

Goodbye Grandma   7

Ode to My Stress Ball   8

Something Splendid   9

I Heard You When You Lied   11

If You Have to Say Goodbye   12

J. T. Never Will Be Ten   13

Were You Ever Fat Like Me?   19

Even Me   25

Countdown to Recess   27

Homework   28

I Called My Teacher Mommy   29

A Fire Drill in My Underwear   30

They Put a Band-Aid on My Head   31

When They Call Me Bad Names   32

I Will Never Crumble   33

When a Friend Moves Away   36

I Cannot Leave on the Last Day of School   37

The Shark on the Playground   39

The Most Important Time   42

Four Wishes   48

The Book That Made Danny Cry   54

Why I'm Late for School   56

Looking in the Mirror at *Didn't Do*   57

They Only See the Outside   58

Introducing a New Me

There's a new ME this year,
an on-time ME,
a clean-desk ME,
a first-to-hand-in-assignments ME,
a listens-in-class-to-the-teacher ME,
a teacher's-pet-for-the-first-time-in-my-life ME,
an always-willing-to-be-good-and-help-out ME,
a dead-serious-get-the-work-done-and-hand-it-in-*before*-it's-due ME.

The problem is
the new ME
is not like ME
at all.

Don't Tell Me

Don't tell me
I won't fail,
for it might
not be true.

Just tell me
you'll still
love me
even if I do.

2

On the Day My Dog Died

On the day
my dog died,

I cried
and cried
and cried.

This is my
whole poem.
There's nothing
more to say.

I cried
and cried
and cried

on the day
my dog died.

Talking to the Mirror in the Bathroom

Someone did something
really bad to me.
"You must tell a grown-up,"
said the lady on TV.

Should I tell my teacher,
Mirror Mirror on the wall?
The principal, the counselor,
the librarian, Mrs. Fall?

Should I tell a friend,
Mirror Mirror tell me true?
Or Mrs. Kay in music,
would she know what to do?

I've made my decision.
I'm walking down the hall.
The books are here to help me,
and so is Mrs. Fall.

We Giggle the Same

I speak English.
Pedro speaks Spanish.

But when we
giggle,

    we

        giggle

           THE SAME!

The Fight

The pencil and eraser
were in a horrid fight.
It went on through the day
and well into the night.

The pencil wrote a message,
"You're just a parasite!"
The eraser erased the message,
not a word was left in sight.

The pencil wrote a sign,
"Erasers cannot write!"
The eraser erased the sign
and did it with delight.

The pencil sent a warning,
"Keep erasers out of sight!"
The eraser erased the warning,
and did it out of spite.

The pencil and the eraser
fought all through the night
and when the morning came
they had disappeared from sight!

Goodbye Grandma

I won't see you ever again.

I won't talk with you ever again.

I won't giggle with you ever again.

I won't eat peaches with you ever again.

But I will miss you

for the rest of my life,

again and again and again and again and again.

Ode to My Stress Ball

This spelling test I have to take.
I'll squish you in an ugly shape.

I'm tired of math and feeling blue,
I'll poke a hundred holes in you.

My hands are bored; what will they do?
They'll make a monster out of you.

Oh, gushy, mushy glob of dough,
there's something that you need to know . . .

In school,
I don't know what I'd do
if I couldn't play with you.

Something Splendid

David ripped
two legs from
a daddy longlegs
he found on the playground.
The legs shook
for a few minutes
and then stopped forever.

David smiled
like a lizard,
and when I wasn't looking,
he put those legs
on my desk
and waited for me to scream.
But I didn't.
I looked at those legs
and imagined
how just this morning
they worked
with six other legs,
on a body
that snuggled so close
to the ground
it could probably hear
the earth's heartbeat.

That daddy longlegs

could see

and hear

and feel,

and maybe even think,

or dream

about a world

we can't even imagine.

If David worked

his entire lifetime,

he probably

couldn't make

something . . .

as splendid!

I Heard You When You Lied

I saw the toy
YOU tried to hide,

and I heard YOU
when YOU lied.

I know the truth,
I really do,

I'm always here
because,

      I'm YOU!

If You Have to Say Goodbye

When you have to say goodbye
to a friend who moved away,
or a pet that died,
you will have to buy a teddy bear
that is the most squeezable one
in the whole store.

When the sad goodbye
hurts too much,
you'll need
to wrap your arms
around that teddy bear,
and squeeze,
and squeeze,
and hug,
and hug,
and cry,
and cry,
until it stops hurting
so much,
and you feel
better.

J. T. Never Will Be Ten

J.T.'s only nine years old.
He never will be ten.
J.T. died today.
They say he had
a very rare disease
that only one person
in a million
ever gets.

From the beginning
of J.T.'s life
his parents knew
he had it.
But I didn't know.

I know I will miss J.T.,
my friend
since grade one.

I'll miss the way he made paper airplanes
and threw them so they flew the highest.
I'll miss the way his glasses
fell down on his nose.
I'll miss how his ears stuck out
from under his baseball cap,
and how he was a fast and a clean player.
I'll miss his phone calls.
"Ben, I can't get those arithmetic problems again,
can you come and *help*?"

And
"Ben,
wanna go camping in my backyard?
We could use my tent
with the big hole in it
so we can see the stars."

Even when I'm ninety-four
I'll still remember him,

J.T.,

my friend

who never will be ten.

Why J.T.?

It's not fair to die

when you're only

nine years old.

But if someone had to die,

why not me

or Jessie or Sally

or Rick or Sue or John?

Why J.T.?

J.T.'s parents gave me

a special box from his room.

He always kept it

on the highest shelf

and the treasures inside

were *our* secret.

I will put

all my memories

of J.T.

in that box,

and every time

I open it . . .

I will see

the freckles on his nose,

hear his yells

as he slid into home base,

and remember

how his laughter

filled the night air

till I broke down

and giggled too.

I will feel

as if my best friend

is sitting beside me,

and I will not be sad,

even for one second,

until I close the box.

Goodbye J.T.

No matter what happens
in my whole life
I will take good care
of your treasure box,

and as long as there are stars
in the night sky
I will hear you laughing.

Were You Ever Fat Like Me?

One day I asked my teacher
a very important question
while she was marking
our arithmetic books.

I had waited a long time
because I was scared
of the answer.

I loved Ms. Danforth,
and I knew that if she had been
a child like me,
I might grow up to be
an adult like her.

My heart was racing
and my hands stuck to the papers
as I placed my arithmetic
in front of her.

I swallowed hard
and hoped nobody would
come to the desk.

"Ms. Danforth," I said,

in a voice that was as soft

as a butterfly's wing.

"When you were a child

were you ever . . . ever . . . fat like me?"

Ms. Danforth stopped marking

red checks on my papers

and looked up.

She adjusted her glasses.

Then she leaned back in her chair,

and I knew she was thinking

with pictures in her mind.

I love Ms. Danforth because

her pictures and my pictures

are often the same.

"Sandra," she said very slowly,

"I was very thin when I was your age.

I was as thin as a toothpick."

"Oh, Ms. Danforth, you were thin!" I cried.
"I always hoped
you had been fat
like me."

My heart dropped to my feet;
I could feel it fall.

Then she said, "Sandra,
when I was in fifth grade
I caught a virus
and an ugly brown rash
grew all over
my arms and legs.

"That's how I was given
the nickname, 'Scabs,'
and that hurt like nothing else."

"'Scabs,'" I said,
imagining her soft skin
covered in an awful rash.
"That must have felt terrible."

"It was itchy, too."
She sighed.
"And very uncomfortable.
Sometimes I felt as if
a thousand ants
were crawling all over me.
In the evenings
I spent hours in the bathtub
so I could have a rest
from all the itching."

"But the scabs are all gone now,"
I said.
"You're lucky."

"Yes," she said,
"By the end of the year
the rash was all gone,
but for the rest of my time

in that school,
I was still 'Scabs.'

"Even today,
there is a part of me
that will always be
'Scabs.'

"When my classmates
called me that name,
I felt as if they were throwing
darts into my heart."

"I know the feeling," I agreed.
"Sometimes by the time I get home,
I feel like a pincushion
that has so many holes
the stuffing is falling out."

Ms. Danforth sighed again.
"It's painful," she said,
"to be called Fatso
or Scabs
or Goody-two Shoes
or Shorty.

"It's all painful."

"It's painful,"
I whispered to myself,
"very painful."

I don't know why,
but I suddenly felt as light
as an autumn leaf.

Even Me

I am a refugee.

It means I came here

to get away from

the country

where I was born

because it was hurting me.

I didn't go to school.

I didn't learn to read.

I didn't have books or pencils.

I didn't color or write.

Now I am a refugee,

in a new country where

everyone goes to school . . .

Even me.

Everyone holds a book

in their hands

and read the words . . .

Even me.

Everyone has crayons and pencils
and they can all draw and write . . .

Even me.

In my old country,
I could not dream
to be a teacher
or a doctor
or a scientist
or an artist
or even to go to school.

I knew these dreams
would never be real.

But in my new country,
everyone can dream,
and work hard,
to make their dreams come true,

Even me.

Countdown to Recess

Sun climbs,
wind chimes.
Five minutes until recess.

A baseball glove,
a game I love.
Four minutes until recess.

I whisper to Pat,
"Get ready to bat."
Three minutes until recess.

My work's all done,
I gotta run.
Two minutes until recess.

Clock, hurry!
Hands, scurry!
One minute until recess.

Brrrrrrrrrrrrrrrrrrrrrrrrrring!

Dash!

Gone in a flash!

Homework

I'm a monster
with a giant mouth.
I devour your playtime,
and then I burp up
a clock
that says,

"GO TO BED!"

I Called My Teacher Mommy

I called my teacher
Mommy.
What a silly thing
I said!

I called my teacher
Mommy.
I have fluff
inside my head!

I called my teacher
Mommy.
Now my face

is apple red!

A Fire Drill in My Underwear

At recess I sit on
a hill of ants,
and now they're crawling
all over my pants.

I run to the bathroom
and hide in the stall.
I take off my pants,
and ants start to fall.

They're crawling all over
the bathroom floor
when the firebell rings
and I race out the door.

Now,
I'm standing outside
in the cold frosty air.
I'm standing outside

in my underwear!

They Put a Band-Aid on My Head

They put a Band-Aid on my head
and said I wasn't well.
They sent me to a special class
to read and write and spell.

I felt as if my brain
was as sick as it could be,
until I met the teacher
who changed my life for me.

In her class we talked a lot,
we read, we wrote, we played,
and slowly, oh so slowly,
the pain began to fade.

When she took the Band-Aid off,
I was shocked to find,
there wasn't a bruise
or even a scar,
no sore of any kind.

When They Call Me Bad Names

T   tears, too tiny for you to see.

E   each one cries inside of me.

A   always try to look okay,

R   right through an awful day.

S   sadness like a cloud of rain,

and tomorrow it starts all over again.

I Will Never Crumble

I'm in a wheelchair.

My dad is too.

I want to ride a bike.

I want to hike.

I want to run in the wind.

I want to play soccer.

But I can't.

I ask my dad,

"Why me?

             Why us?"

My dad says,

"Why NOT us?

Life is unfair,

but we must go on anyway.

It's your choice to grumble,

and then crumble up

like an old muffin,

or to discover
 all that you still can do,
and then do it."

It's not fair that life's unfair,
but my dad is right,
and I will

        never

            ever

crumble up like an old muffin.

When a Friend Moves Away

You stop smiling.

You stop laughing.

Nothing's funny anymore.

You keep looking.

You keep hoping

that you'll see him once more.

You keep wishing.

You keep dreaming

he'll come right through the door.

I Cannot Leave on the Last
Day of School

I want my teacher
to know,
SHE'S MY FAVORITE,
AND I CANNOT GO!

The last day of school
is in sight,
but I'm hanging on
with all my might.

To the year that was
the best by far,
and dazzled with
a zillion stars.

To the year that should
end with cheers,
and not with these
big soggy tears.

I want my teacher
to know,
SHE'S MY FAVORITE,
AND I CANNOT GO!

The Shark on the Playground

Tim is a bully.

He hogs the slide.

He won't let anyone on the climbing bars.

He grabs soccer balls and skipping ropes

and won't give them back.

He throws stones and he hits.

The little kids are all afraid of him,

and some of the big kids are too.

He's like the great white shark

of our playground.

We need to make this

STOP!

We form a group

and have three rules.

        Don't show fear.

        Stand our ground.

        Be strong.

When he's being mean
to the little kids on the slide,
we surround it
and together we yell,

    Get off!

He looks at nine of us,
and knows he is outnumbered.
He gets off the slide,
and goes to the climbing bars.

"LEAVE,"
he tells the little kids.
and they all jump off
and run away
as fast as they can.

We surround the climbing bars.
This time there are fifteen of us.

    Get off!

He is outnumbered again.

Whenever Tim does something mean,
we surround him,
Twenty . . . thirty . . . forty . . .
of us,

and one day
the big white shark
of our playground
swims away,
and never comes back.

Tim is left behind,
and he's just a boy,
a fourth-grade boy,
who knows he can't be mean,

Anymore.

The Most Important Time

One day, my teacher, Ms. Barber,
asked us to be reporters.
"Here is your question to research,"
she said.
"What is the most important time
in a person's life?"

One team asked the principal.
"Mrs. Rawl, what is the
most important time
in a person's life?"

Mrs. Rawl rubbed her chin and said,
"That is a very difficult question.
Perhaps, it is when one is old
and has great wisdom."

One team asked
the lady in the office.
"Ms. Price, what is
the most important time
in a person's life?"

Ms. Price stopped working
on her computer and replied,
"That is a very difficult question.
Perhaps it is when one first becomes
a mother or a father."

One team asked Mr. Bergman,
the music teacher,
"What is the most important time
in a person's life?"

Mr. Bergman put down
his trombone and said,
"That is a very difficult question.
But, I think it is when a person
first learns to love music."

The last team asked
the custodian, Mr. Lenz,
"What is the most important time
in a person's life?"

Mr. Lenz stopped piling boxes
in the storage closet and said,
"That is a very difficult question.
I think it might be when you create
something beautiful,
like a poem or a painting or a garden."

We returned to our classroom
and Ms. Barber asked,
"Did anyone answer your question?"

Each team reported
on the answers they received.

Then Melanie had a suggestion.
"Why don't you ask us?
We might know the answer."

"Of course," said Ms. Barber.
"Of course I should ask YOU."

Then she said,
"What is the most important time
in a person's life?"

Matthew was so excited
that his hand shot up
like a rocket
and before the teacher
could pick someone to reply,
he yelled,

"That's an easy question!
I know the answer."

"Then what is it?" asked Ms. Barber.

Matthew replied,
"It's right now, of course.
It's today!
Why, Jessica brought her dancing soda bottle
for sharing time,
and Terry had his first basket in the gym,
and Susie fell out of her chair
three times in a row,
and there's a bird peeking
in the classroom window
right this instant,
and he's looking at us
as if he wants to go to school."

We all looked at the bird
and he looked at us,
and then we grew as quiet
as a school on a summer day.

Finally Ms. Barber softly said,
"Thank you, Matthew.
Thank you for giving us
the perfect answer
to this question."

Four Wishes

I made four wishes
on the day
my fifth-grade teacher
took us on a field trip
to the top of a mountain.

As the school bus
left the city,
it drove past
rows of shops,
miles of concrete,
and acres of apartment buildings . . .

until,
like a fading dream,
the city was left behind.

My window was dirty,
so I rubbed it
with a tissue
and then squished my nose
against it
so I could see.

Someone planted
a zillion trees out there,
and I wanted to pick
the one that was so bushy
it could hide me
like a secret,
inside its branches.

That's when I made
my first wish.

I wished I could take home that tree
and plant it outside
my classroom window
so I could rest
in its branches
at recess.

And sometimes
I could climb to the top
and look
through the smog
to see if the sun
was still there.

Then I saw the flowers!
Two zillion, in colors
I had never seen before,
and right away
I changed my wish.

Instead of one tree,
I wished
I could bring back
a field of flowers
to run in at lunchtime.

But then I saw the river
and it was deeper
than any blue
I had ever seen,
and I knew
that in all my collection
of seventy-eight crayons
there wasn't a single one
that could color this river.
So I had to change my wish,
again.

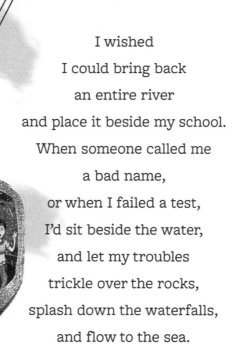

I wished
I could bring back
an entire river
and place it beside my school.
When someone called me
a bad name,
or when I failed a test,
I'd sit beside the water,
and let my troubles
trickle over the rocks,
splash down the waterfalls,
and flow to the sea.

But then we rode a gondola
to the top of the world
where it was so quiet
that I could hear
the winds whispering
and one bird,
singing to an audience
of mountain peaks
sprinkled with snow
like sugar.

Then, I made
my last and final wish.

I wished
I could bring back
the whole mountain,
and place my school
at the very top,
with the whispering winds
and the frosted mountain peaks.

Every day,
I'd ride a gondola
to my school
at the top of the world.

Of course,
these were only wishes,
and all too soon,
we had to ride back down again,
and board the bus,
and pass the river,
and the flowers,
and the trees,
and soon we were home again
in our concrete world.

But sometimes,

when I sit at my desk at school,

and close my eyes a certain way,

I can see

the mountain peaks,

and the flowers and the trees,

and I can hear

the winds and the river

rushing on to the ocean.

Then I know

that I have

all of that beauty

inside of me,

and that all my wishes

have come true.

The Book That Made Danny Cry

It is quiet reading time.
Everyone in class is reading,
except Danny.

He's crying.

I've never seen
Danny cry before—
not even when
he broke his arm
during recess.

"What's wrong, Danny?"
the teacher asks.

Danny can't talk.
He points to a page
in his book.

"Ah," says the teacher.
"I've read that book too,
and you must be on the
last chapter."

Danny sniffs and nods.

The teacher pats him
on the head and says,

"Sometimes good books
are very sad,
because life is often sad."

Danny sniffs and nods again.

I sit at my desk
and wonder what book
Danny is reading.

I want to read that book—

The book that made Danny cry!

Why I'm Late for School

The warlock put me in his pot,

and sprinkled pepper on my nose,

and strange seasonings on my toes,

but little did he know

that pepper makes me *sneeze!*

Ah! Chouuuuuuuuuuuuuuuuuuuuuuuuu!

I blew him like a rocket,

far into the milky way,

and climbed out of his grimy pot,

to be late for school today!

Looking in the Mirror at *Didn't Do*

I shudda finished my spelling.
I wudda finished my spelling.
I cudda finished my spelling.

But wudda
jumped on cudda,
and shudda
jumped on wudda,

and then all three
were toppled over
by

DIDN'T DO!

They Only See the Outside

On the outside, I'm just Benjie,
shortest boy in grade four,
just a hiccup in this classroom
that everyone ignores.

Dragon Daydream

But if a dragon came
and tried to eat our class,
I'd rush the children out,
till I was at the last.
Then I'd fight that dragon,
with my trusty sword,
and I'd end his blazing furies
so we'd be safe once more.

Romeo Daydream

I know that if I was picked
to act in Shakespeare's play,
I'd turn into Romeo,
in a most gallant way,
and at the tragic ending,
when "With a kiss I die,"
everyone would be in tears,
everyone would cry.

Hockey Daydream

I know if I was given
skates and a hockey puck,
and plopped on an icy rink
with just a touch of luck,
everyone would cheer me on,
"Look at Ben out there,
he's faster than a bolt of light,
other team, beware!"

They only see the outside,
not the inside part of me,
but what I'd give for the chance
to set the inside free.

Kalli Dakos is a children's poet and educator. She visits schools across the United States and Canada to encourage children and teachers to write about their own lives. She has written many collections of school poems that include six ILA/CBC Children's Choice Selections, such as *If You're Not Here, Please Raise Your Hand*. She lives in Ottawa, Canada, and has an office in Ogdensburg, NY.
Visit kallidakos.com

Jimothy Oliver is an illustrator who produces commissioned work for clients worldwide. He has worked as a freelance illustrator since 1995 including a stint working as an in-house illustrator at Elsevier in London. He lives in the UK.

Magination Press is the children's book imprint of the American Psychological Association. APA works to advance psychology as a science and profession and as a means of promoting health and human welfare. Magination Press books reach young readers and their parents and caregivers to make navigating life's challenges a little easier. It's the combined power of psychology and literature that makes a Magination Press book special.
Visit maginationpress.org
⧉ 𝕏 ⧉ ⧉ @MaginationPress